For Pandora
J.N.

For Sam's Mum
P. H.

Walter Lorraine 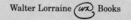 Books

Text copyright © Jenny Nimmo 1999
Illustrations copyright © Paul Howard 1999

First American edition 2000
Originally published in Great Britain 1999
by Methuen Children's Books
an imprint of Egmont Children's Books Limited
239 Kensington High Street, London W8 6SA

Library of Congress Cataloging-in-Publication Data
Nimmo, Jenny.
Esmeralda and the children next door / Jenny Nimmo : illustrated
by Paul Howard.
p. cm.
Summary: Esmeralda can lift her parents high in the air but the
children next door, whom Esmeralda would like to play with, are
scared of her size and strength.
ISBN 0-618-02902-8
[1. Friendship Fiction.] I. Howard, Paul, 1967- ill.
II. Title.
PZ7.N5897Es 2000
[E]-DC21   99-28563
                                                              CIP

Printed in UAE
by Oriental Press Limited
10 9 8 7 6 5 4 3 2 1

Esmeralda
and the
Children Next Door

Jenny Nimmo

Paul Howard

HOUGHTON MIFFLIN COMPANY, BOSTON 2000

Walter Lorraine Books

Esmeralda was a very large baby. When she was only six months old she chewed right through the bars of her crib.

"Esmeralda will be a strong woman," her dad said. "She can join us in the circus."

When Esmeralda was four years old she could lift an armchair.

Her mom made her a leopard-skin top and a frilly skirt.

But the children next door wouldn't play with Esmeralda.

"You're a giant," they said. "You would hurt us."

And they wouldn't let Esmeralda hold their toys.
"You're too clumsy," they said. "You would break them."

When Esmeralda was six she could carry
her mom and dad on her shoulders.

The children next door wouldn't even let
Esmeralda go near their cat.

"You're too strong," they said. "You would crush her."

When Esmeralda was seven her mom and dad said,
"Esmeralda, soon you can join our circus act.
You are a strong woman now."

They thought this would make their daughter happy.

But Esmeralda didn't want to be a strong woman.
She wanted to be an acrobat or a tightrope walker.
She didn't like eating meat every day, or wearing animal
skins or lifting weights.

"Strong women eat meat to make them grow," her dad said. "They lift weights to keep them strong and they wear animal skins to show they are as tough as lions."

So Esmeralda ate her meat and lifted weights and wore a leopard-skin, but she was very unhappy. She grew so big the children next door ran away from her.

Alone in her room, Esmeralda made beautiful paper
animals and sang to them.
They were her only friends.

But the children next door called out, "Esmeralda sings like a frog!" never guessing that she had gentle, clever fingers and a heart of gold.

In the summer Esmeralda and
her family went on tour.
  They performed in cities
all round the world.

  Esmeralda carried her
parents on her shoulders.

  She threw them in the
air and caught them.

She bent iron bars
with her teeth

and pretended
to enjoy lifting rocks.

The crowds loved her!

But at night when Mom and Dad were sleeping in their brightly painted caravan, Esmeralda would gaze at the moon and think about the children next door.

When autumn came, the tour ended and the family returned home.

Mom and Dad cooked a special supper to celebrate their first night home, but Esmeralda didn't enjoy it. When she went to bed, she didn't sing to her paper animals. She was too sad.

In the morning Esmeralda ran to peep in the garden
next door.

The children had a new baby sister. Esmeralda longed to
hold her, but the children shouted, "Go away, Esmeralda.
You'll frighten the baby."

The next day a wind swept into the village.
Esmeralda ran outside and watched the clouds tearing
through the sky. The wind was as fierce and strong
as she was.

"Come and play with me," she cried. "No one else will."

But the wind rushed past Esmeralda and into the
branches of the tree next door. The tree shuddered
and a great branch cracked.

The baby next door was fast asleep in her pram under the tree. The children next door looked out of the window and saw the branch was going to crush their baby. They all rushed out of the house, but they were too scared to go near the tree.

Esmeralda leapt over the wall and caught the branch as it fell. She pushed the branch away from the baby and it crashed to the ground beside the pram. Esmeralda felt her great strength leaving her.

The children next door tiptoed over to the girl lying in the grass.

"She doesn't look frightening anymore," they said. Esmeralda's dad ran out to see what had happened.

"She saved our baby," called the children next door. "How can we thank her?"

Esmeralda's mom put her in bed and waited for her to get better.

The doctor came and shook his head. "It seems Esmeralda doesn't want to get strong again," he said.

Esmeralda lay in bed all winter.
She never saw the children next door skating,
tobogganing and snowballing.

Sometimes they looked up
at Esmeralda's window. They
wondered where she was.
They missed her.

When the trees began to blossom, Mom said, "We can't go on tour without Esmeralda. What shall we do?"

"Perhaps it's time we asked the children next door," suggested Dad.

The children next door were sorry to hear Esmeralda was still ill and went to visit her.

They saw all the paper animals so neatly and cleverly made.

"How beautiful," they whispered. "We wish we could make paper animals."

The children crept close to Esmeralda. They put their toys, their cat and their baby on her bed.

"Please get strong, Esmeralda," they said. "We want you to come and play with us."

Esmeralda gave a tiny smile. Only the baby saw it.

The next day, Esmeralda sat up in bed.

"What a lovely day, "she said. "What's for breakfast?"

Then Esmeralda gathered up her paper animals, opened the window and threw them into the air.

"For you!" she cried to the children next door.

"Hurrah!" they shouted as they ran to catch the floating creatures. "Esmeralda is well again."

Esmeralda is still with the circus but she's not the strong woman anymore.

Every summer she goes round the world with her mom and dad.

She swings high on the trapeze and walks the tightrope.

The crowds stare in amazement and gasp at her bravery.

Esmeralda loves it.

But in the autumn she comes home to play with the children next door.

They say she's the best friend they've ever had.